A BABY SISTER FOR FRANCES

by RUSSELL HOBAN

Pictures by LILLIAN HOBAN

HarperCollins*Publishers*

A BABY SISTER FOR FRANCES
Text copyright © 1964 by Russell Hoban; renewed 1992 by Russell Hoban
Illustrations copyright © 1964, 1993 by Lillian Hoban; renewed 1992 by Lillian Hoban
Printed in the U.S.A. All rights reserved.

Library of Congress Cataloging-in-Publication Data
Hoban, Russell.
  A baby sister for Frances / by Russell Hoban ; pictures by Lillian Hoban.
    p. cm.
  Summary: When things change around the house after her baby sister is born, Frances
decides to run away—but not too far.
    ISBN 0-06-022335-9. — ISBN 0-06-022336-7 (lib. bdg.)
    ISBN 0-06-443006-5 (pbk.)
    [1. Badgers—Fiction. 2. Babies—Fiction. 3. Sisters—Fiction. 4. Family life—
Fiction.] I. Hoban, Lillian, ill. II. Title.
PZ7.H637Bab   1993   92-32603
[E]—dc20   CIP
                                           AC

❖
Newly Illustrated Edition

For Barbara Alexandra Dicks,
who often signs her name in lower case
but is, in fact, a capital person

It was a quiet evening.
Father was reading his newspaper.
Mother was feeding Gloria, the new baby.
Frances was sitting under the kitchen sink.
She was singing a little song:

Plinketty, plinketty, plinketty, plink,
Here is the dishrag that's under the sink.
Here are the buckets and brushes and me,
Plinketty, plinketty, plinketty, plee.

She stopped the song and listened.
Nobody said anything.

Frances went to her room and took some gravel
out of the drawer where she had been saving it.
She put the gravel into her empty coffee can
and put the lid back on the can.
Frances marched into the living room
and rattled the gravel in the can.
As she marched she sang a marching song:

Here we go marching, rattley bang!

"Please don't do that, Frances," said Father.
Frances stopped.
"All right," she said.
She went back to the kitchen and sat down under the sink.
Mother came in, carrying Gloria.
"Why are you sitting under the sink?" said Mother.
"I like it here," said Frances. "It's cozy."
"Would you like to help me put Gloria to bed?" said Mother.

"How much allowance does Gloria get?" said Frances.
"She is too little to have an allowance," said Father.
"Only big girls like you get allowances.
Isn't it nice to be a big sister?"
"May I have a penny along with my nickel
now that I am a big sister?" said Frances.
"Yes," said Father. "Now your allowance
will be six cents a week because you are a big sister."
"Thank you," said Frances.
"I know a girl who gets seventeen cents a week.
She gets three nickels and two pennies."
"Well," said Father, "it's time for bed now."
Father picked Frances up from under the sink
and gave her a piggyback ride to bed.

Mother and Father tucked her in and kissed her good night.
"I need my tiny special blanket," said Frances.
Mother gave her the tiny special blanket.
"And I need my tricycle and my sled
and both teddy bears
and my alligator doll," said Frances.
Father brought in the tricycle and the sled
and both teddy bears and the alligator doll.
Mother and Father kissed her good night again
and Frances went to sleep.

In the morning Frances got up and washed
and began to dress for school.
"Is my blue dress ready for me to wear?" said Frances.
"Oh, dear," said Mother, "I was so busy with Gloria
that I did not have time to iron it,
so you'll have to wear the yellow one."
Mother buttoned Frances up the back.
Then she brushed her hair and put a new ribbon in it
and put her breakfast on the table.
"Why did you put sliced bananas on the oatmeal?"
said Frances.
"Did you forget that I like raisins?"
"No, I did not forget," said Mother,
"but you finished up the raisins yesterday
and I have not been out shopping yet."

"Well," said Frances, "things are not very good
around here anymore. No clothes to wear.
No raisins for the oatmeal.
I think maybe I'll run away."
"Finish your breakfast," said Mother.
"It is almost time for the school bus."
"What time will dinner be tonight?" said Frances.
"Half past six," said Mother.
"Then I will have plenty of time to run away
after dinner," said Frances,
and she kissed her mother good-bye
and went to school.

After dinner that evening
Frances packed her little knapsack very carefully.
She put in her tiny special blanket and her alligator doll.
She took all of the nickels and pennies
out of her bank, for travel money,
and she took her good luck coin for good luck.
Then she took a box of prunes from the kitchen
and five chocolate sandwich cookies.

"Well," said Frances, "it is time to say good-bye.
I am on my way. Good-bye."
"Where are you running away to?" said Father.
"I think that under the dining-room table is the best place,"
said Frances. "It's cozy,
and the kitchen is near if I run out of cookies."
"That is a good place to run away to," said Mother,
"but I'll miss you."
"I'll miss you too," said Father.
"Well," said Frances, "good-bye," and she ran away.

Father sat down with his newspaper.
Mother took up the sweater she was knitting.
Father put down the newspaper.
"You know," he said, "it is not the same house without Frances."
"That is just *exactly* what I was thinking," said Mother.
"The place seems lonesome and empty without her."
Frances sat under the dining-room table and ate her prunes.
"Even Gloria," said Mother, "as small as she is,
can feel the difference."
"I can hear her crying a little right now," said Father.
"Well," said Mother, "a girl looks up to an older sister.
You know that."

Father picked up his newspaper.
Then he put it down again.
"I miss the songs that Frances used to sing," he said.
"I was *so* fond of those little songs," said Mother.
"Do you remember the one about the tomato?
'What does the tomato say, early in the dawn?'" sang Mother.
"'Time to be all red again, now that night is gone,'" sang Father.
"Yes," he said, "that is a good one, but my favorite

has always been: 'When the wasps and the bumblebees
have a party, nobody comes that can't buzz. . . .'"
"Well," said Mother, "we shall just have to
get used to a quiet house now."

Frances ate three of the sandwich cookies
and put the other two aside for later.
She began to sing:

> *I am poor and hungry here, eating prunes and rice.*
> *Living all alone is not really very nice.*

She had no rice, but chocolate sandwich cookies
did not sound right for the song.

"I can almost hear her now," said Father,
humming the tune that Frances had just sung.
"She has a charming voice."
"It is just not a *family* without Frances," said Mother.
"Babies are very nice. Goodness knows I *like* babies,
but a baby is not a family."
"Isn't that a fact!" said Father.
"A family is *everybody all together*."

"Remember," said Mother, "how I used to say,
'Think how lucky the new baby will be
to have a sister like Frances'?"
"I remember that very well," said Father,
"and I hope that Gloria turns out
to be as clever and good as Frances."
"With a big sister like Frances to help her along,
she ought to turn out just fine," said Mother.
"I'd like to hear from Frances," said Father,
"just to know how she is getting along in her new place."
"I'd like to hear from Frances too," said Mother,
"and I'm not sure the sleeves are right
on this sweater I'm knitting for her."

"Hello," called Frances from the dining room.
"I am calling on the telephone. Hello, hello,
this is me. Is that you?"

"Hello," said Mother. "This is us. How are you?"
"I am fine," said Frances. "This is a nice place,
but you miss your family when you're away. How are you?"
"We are all well," said Father, "but we miss you too."
"I will be home soon," said Frances, and she hung up.

"She said that she will be home soon," said Father.
"That is good news indeed," said Mother.
"I think I'll bake a cake."
Frances put on her knapsack and sang
a little traveling song:

Big sisters really have to stay
At home, not travel far away,
Because everybody misses them
And wants to hug-and-kisses them.

"I'm not sure about that last rhyme," said Frances
as she arrived in the living room
and took off her knapsack.
"That's a good enough rhyme," said Father.
"I like it fine," said Mother,
and they both hugged and kissed her.

"What kind of cake are you baking?" said Frances to Mother.

"Chocolate," said Mother.

"It's too bad that Gloria's too little to have some,"
said Frances, "but when she's a big girl like me,
she can have chocolate cake too."

"Oh, yes," said Mother, "you may be sure that
there will always be plenty of chocolate cake around here."

The End